SomeTHING Lives in the Attic!

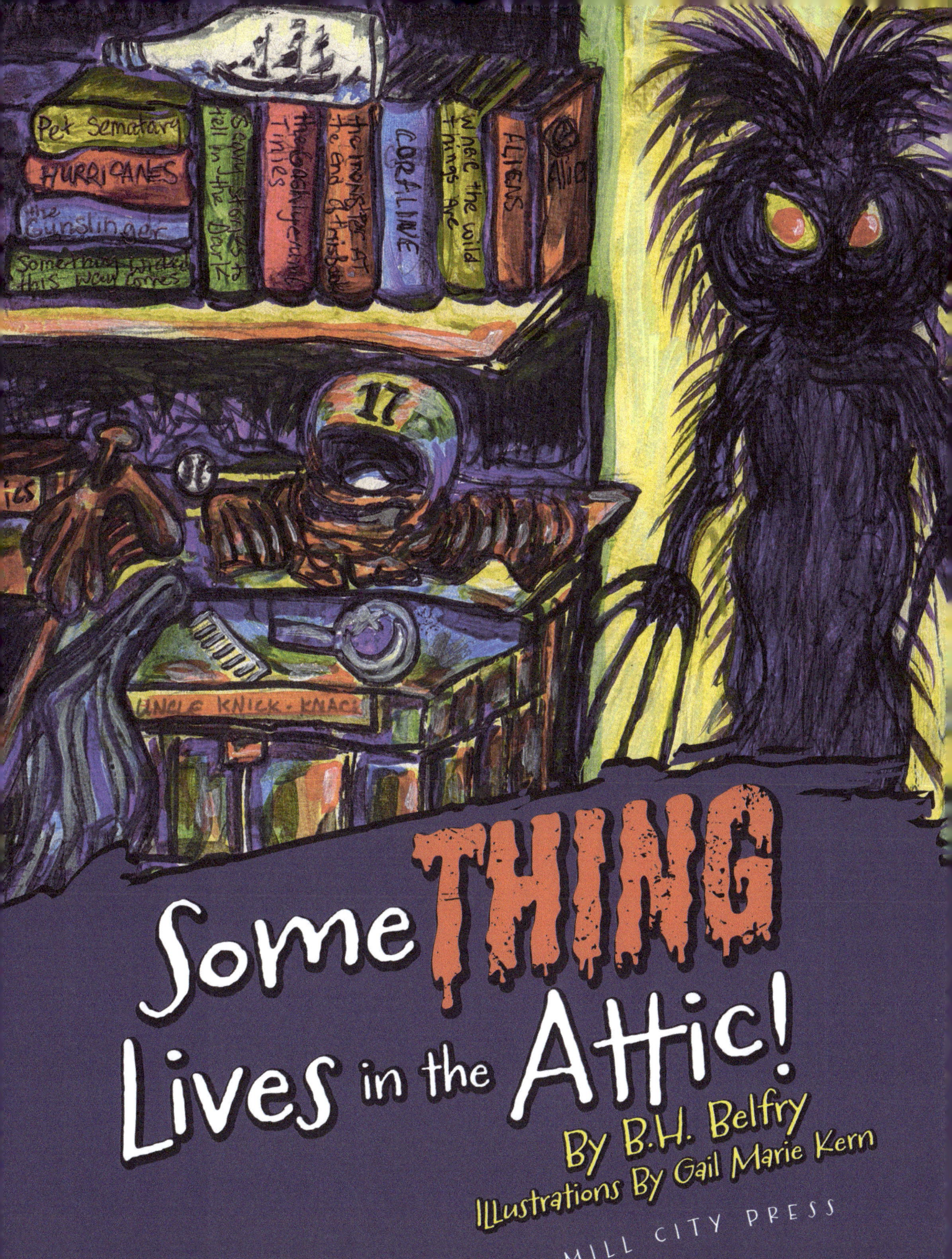

Mill City Press
555 Winderley Pl, Suite 225
Maitland, FL 32751
407.339.4217
www.millcitypress.net

© 2024 by B.H. Belfry

All rights reserved solely by the author. The author guarantees all contents are original and do not infringe upon the legal rights of any other person or work. No part of this book may be reproduced in any form without the permission of the author.

Due to the changing nature of the Internet, if there are any web addresses, links, or URLs included in this manuscript, these may have been altered and may no longer be accessible. The views and opinions shared in this book belong solely to the author and do not necessarily reflect those of the publisher. The publisher therefore disclaims responsibility for the views or opinions expressed within the work.

Paperback ISBN-13: 978-1-66288-564-8
Ebook ISBN-13: 978-1-66288-565-5

Dedication

To Nala Ruby and Esmerelda,
my ruby and emerald.
I promise to always check your room for monsters at bedtime.
—B.H.B.

For my grandmother, Ruth Herbst, who encouraged me to draw.
—G.M.K.

PRAISE for Some THING Lives in the Attic!

"Quirky, creepy, fun – author B.H. Belfry knows how to tell an engaging, rhythmic story that is sure to keep kids on the edge of their seat until the very last page. Not too scary, perfect for quiet reading time or a rollicking read along. Highly recommended for kids and parents, especially for spooky season!"

—TOM LUCAS, Author of *Research Randy and the Mystery of Grandma's Half-eaten Pie of Despair.*

"B.H. Belfry's *Some THING Lives in the Attic!* teems with delightful mischief and wonderful fear as a mystery unfolds with glorious, sonic perplexity."

—JOHN KING, Author of *Guy Psycho and the Ziggurat of Shame.*

"For all scheming siblings and overactive imaginations, this book is perfect spooky fun! Belfry and Kern have teamed up to create a bickering brother-sister duo who creep upward toward the attic of their Victorian home to find an entirely unexpected THING. Great classroom read or family library addition!"

—BETHANY DUVALL, Writer, Educator.

"I am enjoying your illustrations. Such a nice break from the typical cartoon style. Nice loose [brush]strokes and a great color palette...Dang, these are great!"

—ALLEN SHEETS, Freelance Graphic Designer and Professor at Minnesota State University Moorhead.

"A truer yarn could not have been spun, even if we had done it with our own webs. B.H. Belfry gives young readers a fine story about the hidden beauty and power of life up inside a good, dusty attic, with plenty of rafters to build strong fly-catching homes!"

—THE CRAWLEYS, Attic Spiders/Storytellers.

"I really don't need to comb my hair. I like a more natural *bedhead* style."

—WEREWOLF, Hair Stylist.

"The frogs aren't my pets or friends. I just eat them for dinner."

—LAKE MONSTER, Environmentalist.

You won't hear it much as the sun rises for the day,
but it's lurking up there, despite what Mom and Dad say.

Up in the attic, it is scuttling and waiting.
Day turns to night, and I hear its scratchy pacing.

After school, Sis and I watch cartoons on TV,
and I hear its claws scratching the floor above me.

At dinner, I hatch a foolproof plan
to catch and tame the THING, if I can.

I skip the spaghetti, but grab the parmesan cheese,
and ask little Sis, "Would you help me, pretty please?"

She bobs her head "yes," and so seals her fate.
I sprinkle it on her clothes to use her for bait.

Mom and Dad frown and tell me I'm foolish.
"There's no THING up there, nasty and ghoulish."

They say, "You're only making up a story.
There is no THING up there, creepy or gory."

But I can hear it drag, bump, lurch, and thud
on the attic floor, like it was stuck in the mud.

                                    and source of the scares.
                        to the second floor,
            up the stairs,
I grab Dad's fishing net and Sis's arm, then run

I turn the creaky knob on the attic's first door,
and open it a crack, in hopes to see a bit more.

I focus my eyes on the dull sliver of light,
and wish so badly it was a little more bright.

The light hits the attic's wood stairs, tall as a giant.
I nudge Sis to move, but she is stubborn and defiant.

In my head, there are visions of what we may see,
some so scary they make me want to pee.

There has to be a monster making those boards creak,
some THING that turns my knees to jelly, making them weak.

Maybe when we reach the top attic stair,
a werewolf will be there, combing his hair.

Or some THING like a glob of green and black mold, may grab and keep us in its gooey-armed hold.

Maybe some muck monster who crept out of the lake, has made his home hiding behind a rusty rake.

Is it the monster in last year's nightmares when I was six, under my bed, thumping springs... and doing its tricks?

What if it's a vampire, blood dripping from fangs? Scowling in her bed, waiting to sink them in my veins.

Maybe it's a night wraith, claws sharp as knives, reaching out to steal both of our lives.

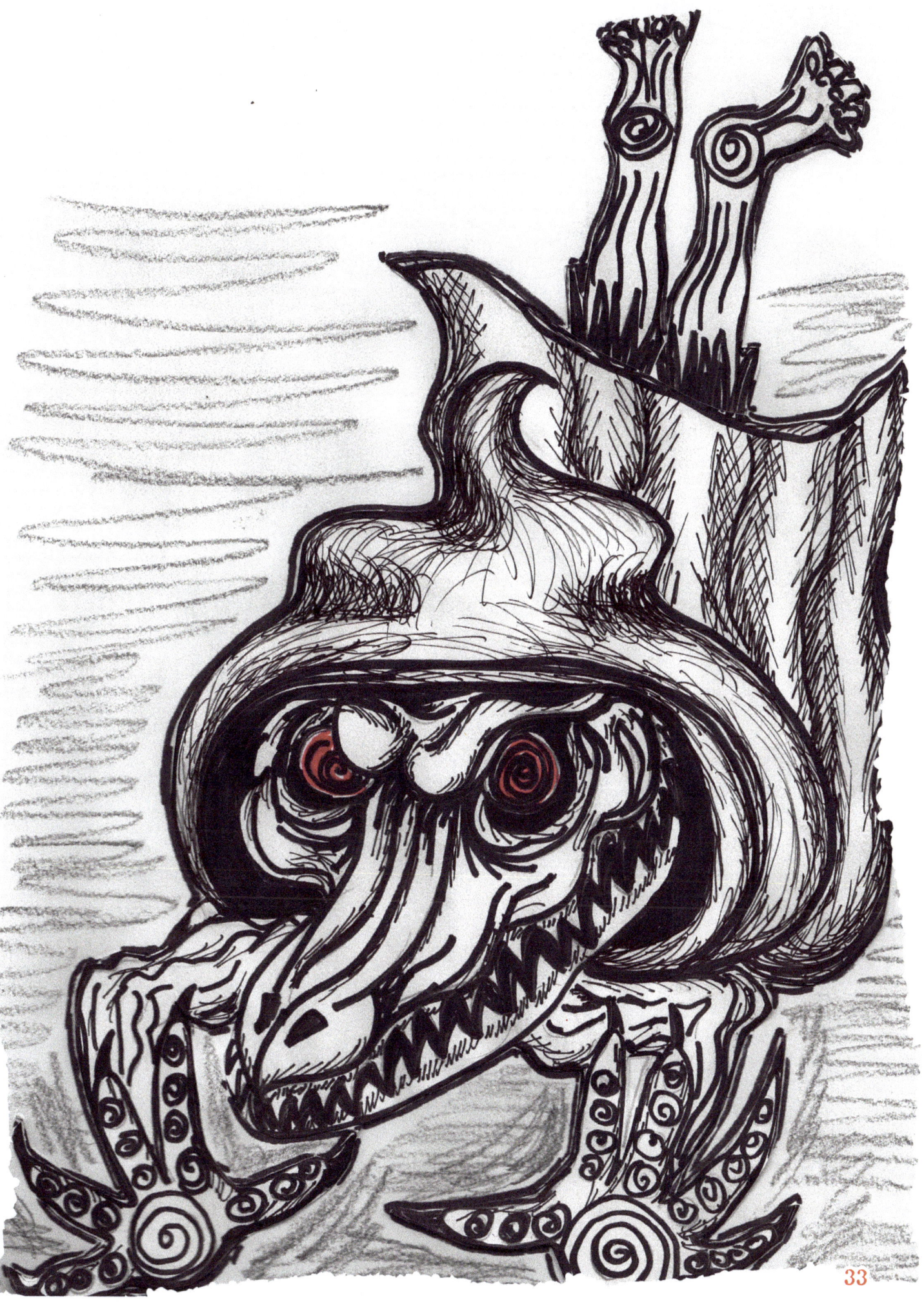

Can it be all the monsters I've seen on TV?
Romping through dusty boxes, at last breaking free?

Whatever it is, I'm going to find out,
even if I'm filled with lots of fear and doubt.

I nudge Sis again to climb that first attic step.
She jumps up but stalls, then loses her pep.

The stairs are dark, except for the sliver of light,
a tall shadow scurries by, then moves out of sight.

I take Sis's hand and raise Dad's old fishing net,
then run up all the stairs to catch a monster pet.

I hear a noisy clatter, and claws on floorboards,
and imagine spooky monsters, coming in hordes.

Past the open door, a hazy shadow climbs the wall,
until it reaches the roof, now over ten feet tall!

Black, fuzzy claws stretch slowly across the room,
rising in the air like an old witch's broom.

They reach out to grab me. I freeze and close my eyes.
Gritting my teeth, I brace to be eaten alive.

But instead of sharp teeth and super long claws,
I hear the light tip-tap of small, furry paws.

Before me, the Some THING is finally here:
A beady-eyed squirrel: the source of my fear!

It sneaks up a rafter with its small peanut-prize.
Sis and I are speechless, jaws dropped in surprise.

She punches my arm. "You dork, I'm going to bed. ALL these stupid monsters are just in your head!"

I follow her downstairs, like a lost little sheep, get into bed, and drift into a safe, deep sleep.

Acknowledgements

This book is indebted to the following, for their collaborative efforts and support:

Inspiration and creative boosts from the Master Muse, and my team at Mill City Press, especially Kim, Ethan, Amanda, and Alicia, for their incredible work, guidance, and design.

Thank you to my knowledgeable, talented friends and critique group beta readers at Shine Street Writers (special thanks for helping me with my rusty rhyme scheme and meter!)

Thank you to the old attic in the house I grew up in for being a properly dusty and creaky one, and full of possibly haunted relics.

Thank you to the many monsters of my youth.

Thank you to *The Addams Family* and Charles Addams.

Thank you, Ray Bradbury, and Edward Gorey, for your words and style.

Thank you to my early readers and encouragers, and family and friends who are always willing to hear another story.

Thank you, Greg C., for talking books with me, and for enthusiastically reading anything I send.

Thank you to all the local spoken word open mics, poetry slams, and wonderful bookstores of Orlando.

Thank you, Tom, Bethany, John, and Allen, for your amazing book blurbs.

Thank you, Claire C., for pushing me to publish and get my writing out in a wide variety of formats, and for checking for monsters underneath *my* bed.

Thank you, Mom, Jolene, Ronda, and my family/friends for being such enthusiastic book promoters, and for all your creative encouragement.

Thank you, Nala, and Esme, for our daily trips into the world of imagination and for showing me how to flex my "play" muscles again. Also, thank you, Nala, for being my very first beta reader and editor. You judged every illustration and word with an excellent editorial eye (and let me know if anything was a little *too* spooky!).

Thank you, Gail, for being a fun and open-minded artist, collaborator, and friend. One of the things I loved most about our process was to see how, when I gave you a few words – often with sparse description – you would come up with something magical, and the back-and-forth brainstorming was a super fun, creative time. You truly brought this little story to life in a dark, poetic, lovely, funny, whimsical, and spooky style.

Last, but definitely not least:
Thank you, Dear Reader, for reading and supporting our work!

Author's Note

Gail and I are an indie artist and author, so if you enjoy this work, please consider leaving a review for us online on Amazon, B&N, Goodreads, or any other online/social media platform of your choice. A review is always one of the best ways to support independent authors and artists, and their work.

Thank you and we hope you enjoy!

Pssst! It's *okay* to sleep with the lights on.

Until next time,
B.H. Belfry
February 2024

Printed in the USA
CPSIA information can be obtained
at www.ICGtesting.com
LVHW071717030424
776198LV00020B/277